ABOUT THE BANK STREET READY-TO-READ SERIES

Seventy years of educational research and innovative teaching have given the Bank Street College of Education the reputation as America's most trusted name in early childhood education.

Because no two children are exactly alike in their development, we have designed the *Bank Street Ready-to-Read* series in three levels to accommodate the individual stages of reading readiness of children ages four through eight.

- ● *Level 1:* GETTING READY TO READ—read-alouds for children who are taking their first steps toward reading.
- ● *Level 2:* READING TOGETHER—for children who are just beginning to read by themselves but may need a little help.
- ○ *Level 3:* I CAN READ IT MYSELF—for children who can read independently.

Our three levels make it easy to select the books most appropriate for a child's development and enable him or her to grow with the series step by step. The *Bank Street Ready-to-Read* books also overlap and reinforce each other, further encouraging the reading process.

We feel that making reading fun and enjoyable is the single most important thing that you can do to help children become good readers. And we hope you'll be a part of Bank Street's long tradition of learning through sharing.

The Bank Street College of Education

W9-DJE-039

To Kate and Alexandra
—J.O.

To Christopher
—L.S.

WAKE UP, BABY!
A Bantam Little Rooster Book
Simultaneous paper-over-board and trade paper editions/September 1990

Little Rooster is a trademark of Bantam Books,
a division of Bantam Doubleday Dell Publishing Group, Inc.

Series graphic design by Alex Jay/Studio J
Associate Editor: Gillian Bucky

Special thanks to James A. Levine, Betsy Gould,
Erin B. Gathrid, and Cheryl Dixon.

All rights reserved.
Copyright © 1990 by Byron Preiss Visual Publications, Inc.
Text copyright © 1990 by Bank Street College of Education.
Illustrations copyright © 1990 by Lynn Sweat and
Byron Preiss Visual Publications, Inc.
No part of this book may be reproduced or transmitted
in any form or by any means, electronic or mechanical,
including photocopying, recording, or by any information
storage and retrieval system, without permission in writing from
the publisher.
For information address: Bantam Books.

Library of Congress Cataloging-in-Publication Data

Oppenheim, Joanne.
Wake up, baby! / by Joanne Oppenheim
illustrated by Lynn Sweat.
p. cm. — (Bank Street ready-to-read)
''A Byron Preiss book.''
''A Bantam little rooster book.''
Summary: Kate's lively and imaginative efforts to wake up the baby
only result in putting Kate to sleep instead.
ISBN 0-553-05907-6. — ISBN 0-553-34914-7 (pbk.)
[1. Babies—Fiction. 2. Sleep—Fiction. 3. Imagination—
Fiction.] I. Sweat, Lynn, ill.
II. Title. III. Series.
PZ7.O616Wak   1990
[E]—dc20

89-38612   CIP   AC

Published simultaneously in the United States and Canada

Bantam Books are published by Bantam Books, a division of Bantam Doubleday
Dell Publishing Group, Inc. Its trademark, consisting of the words ''Bantam Books''
and the portrayal of a rooster, is Registered in U.S. Patent and Trademark Office
and in other countries. Marca Registrada. Bantam Books, 666 Fifth Avenue, New
York, New York 10103.

PRINTED IN THE UNITED STATES OF AMERICA

0 9 8 7 6 5 4 3 2 1

Christine Towne

Bank Street Ready-to-Read™

Wake Up, Baby!

by Joanne Oppenheim
Illustrated by Lynn Sweat

A Byron Preiss Book

A BANTAM LITTLE ROOSTER BOOK

NEW YORK · TORONTO · LONDON · SYDNEY · AUCKLAND

"Can we go now?"
asked Kate.
"Not now," said Kate's mom.
"We can go when the baby
wakes up."

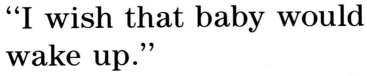

"I wish that baby would wake up."

"I bet you could
wake the baby."

"Is the baby awake yet?"
Kate asked.
"No, Kate," said Mom.
"A herd of elephants
couldn't wake this baby!"

"Is the baby awake yet?"
asked Kate.
"A marching band couldn't
wake this baby," said Mom.

"Could you wake the baby?"

"Is the baby awake yet?"
Kate asked again.
"A five-alarm fire
couldn't wake this baby,"
Kate's mom said.

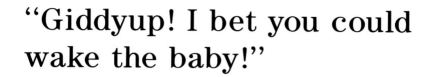

"Giddyup! I bet you could wake the baby!"

"Is the baby awake now?" asked Kate.

"Wild horses couldn't wake this baby," said Kate's mom.

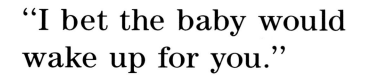

"I bet the baby would wake up for you."

"Is the baby awake now?"
Kate asked.
"Kate, a three-ring circus
couldn't wake this baby,"
said Mom.

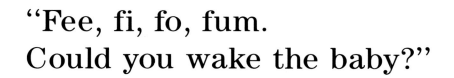

"Fee, fi, fo, fum.
Could you wake the baby?"

"Kate!" called Mom.
"The baby is awake!"

"Now we can go,"
called Mom.

"Kate?" Mom called.

"Wake up, Kate!"